This **Frog** book belongs to:

....

This paperback edition first published in 2014 by Andersen Press Ltd.

20 Vauxhall Bridge Road, London SW1V 2SA.

First published in Great Britain in 1992 by Andersen Press Ltd.

Published in Australia by Random House Australia Pty.,

20 Alfred Street, Milsons Point, Sydney, NSW 2061.

Colour separated in Switzerland by Photolitho AG, Zürich.

Printed and bound in China by Foshan Zhaorong Printing Co., Ltd.

10   9   8   7   6   5   4   3   2   1

British Library Cataloguing in Publication Data available.

ISBN 978 1 78344 147 1

Frog
in Winter

Max Velthuijs

Andersen Press

When Frog got up one morning, he realised at once that something was wrong with the world. Something had changed.

He went to the window and was astonished to see that everything was completely white.

He rushed outside in confusion. There was snow
everywhere. It was slippery under his feet.
Suddenly he felt himself falling over backwards . . .

. . . down the bank, into the river. But the river was frozen and Frog lay on his back on the cold, hard ice. "If there's no water, I won't be able to wash," he thought, shocked.

Shivering with cold he sat on the bank. Then
Duck came hurrying towards him on her skates.
"Hello, Frog," she said. "Nice weather today!
Are you coming skating?"

"No, I'm freezing," replied Frog.
"But skating is good for you," said Duck. "I'll teach you."

So Duck gave Frog her skates and her scarf. She pushed him and he slid quickly across the ice, but not for long. Soon, he fell.
"Aren't you enjoying yourself?" said Duck. But Frog was nearly frozen solid and his teeth were chattering with cold.

"You've got a warm feathery coat, but I'm just a bare frog," he said.
"You're right," said Duck. "You'd better keep my scarf, as I must be on my way."

Then Pig appeared with a basket of firewood
on her back.
"Aren't you freezing, Pig?" asked Frog.
"Freezing?" said Pig. "No! I'm enjoying the fresh,
healthy air. Winter is the most beautiful season."

"You have a nice layer of fat to keep you warm,
but what do I have?" said Frog.
"Poor Frog," thought Pig. "I wish I could help him."

One, two! One, two! Hare ran up. He was jogging
in the snow.
"Hurrah!" he called joyously. "Sport makes you
healthy! Hurrah for sport! Three cheers for sport!"

"Why don't you join in, Frog? It's great fun
keeping fit."
"I'm freezing," said Frog. "You've got warm fur, but
I have nothing." Sadly, he went home.

The next day his friends invited him to have a
snowball fight. But Frog couldn't share in the fun.

"I'm freezing," he murmured. "I'm only a bare frog."
And miserably he stumbled home.

He sat next to the fire for the rest of the day,
dreaming of spring and summer.
He burned every last piece of wood.

When the fire went out, he went outside to gather more logs. But he couldn't find any wood in the snow.

He walked and walked until he lost his way.
Everything was white.
Exhausted, he lay down in the snow.
A bare frog.

And there his friends found him.
"I'm freezing," whispered Frog.
"Come on," said Hare, and carefully they
carried him home and put him to bed.

Hare collected wood and lit a fire. Pig cooked a
hot, nourishing soup and Duck cheered Frog up.

In the evenings that followed, everyone listened while
Hare read wonderful stories about spring and summer.
Pig knitted Frog a warm pullover in two colours. Frog
enjoyed the attention from his friends. Winter is
wonderful when you can spend it in bed!

Then the day came when Frog was well enough to get up. Without fur, fat or feathers, but dressed in his new pullover, he took his first steps in the snow.

"Well?" asked Hare curiously.

"It's good," answered Frog bravely.

So the long winter passed. But one morning, when Frog opened his eyes, he noticed at once that something was different. Bright light streamed in the window. Quickly, he jumped out of bed and ran outside.

The world was bright green and the sun shone in the sky. "Hurray!" he cried. "It's good to be a frog. How wonderful! I can feel the sun's rays on my bare back." His friends were happy to see Frog so cheerful.

"What would we do without Frog?" laughed Hare.
"I can't think," said Pig.
"No," agreed Duck. "Life just wouldn't be the
same without him!"

Max Velthuijs's twelve beautiful stories about **Frog** and his friends first started to appear twenty five years ago and are now available as paperbacks, e-books and apps.

9781783441440 — *Frog is a Hero*
9781783441532 — *Frog and the Birdsong*
9781783441501 — *Frog Finds a Friend*
9781783441426 — *Frog is Frightened*
9781783441471 — *Frog in Winter*
9781783441457 — *Frog in Love*
9781783441525 — *Frog is Sad*
97811783441433 — *Frog and the Stranger*
9781783441518 — *Frog and the Treasure*
9781783441495 — *Frog and a Very Special Day*
9781783441488 — *Frog and the Wide World*
9781783441419 — *Frog is Frog*

Max Velthuijs (Dutch for Field House) lived in the Netherlands, and received the prestigious Hans Christian Andersen Medal for Illustration. His charming stories capture childhood experiences while offering life lessons to children as young as three, and have been translated into more than forty languages.

'Frog is an inspired creation – a masterpiece of graphic simplicity.'
GUARDIAN

'Miniature morality plays for our age.' IBBY